Mint Grows Even In The Dark

Amy Laurens

OTHER WORKS

Find other works by the author at
www.amylaurens.com/books

MINT GROWS EVEN IN THE DARK

Amy Laurens

AUSTRALIA

Print ISBN: 978-1-923305-01-4
eBook ISBN: 9798227469274

www.inkprintpress.com

National Library of Australia Cataloguing-in-Publication Data
Laurens, Amy 1985—
Mint Grows Even In The Dark
58 p.   cm.
ISBN: 978-1-923305-01-4
Inkprint Press, Canberra, Australia
1. Fiction—Fantasy—Contemporary 2. Fiction—Fairy Tales, Folk Tales, Legends & Mythology

Summary: Claire knows where the missing people are—and given no one would believe her if she told them, it's up to her to brave the mysterious cave and get them back.

First Edition: March 2025

Cover design © White Deer Graphic Design
Mint graphics © Canva, used under licence

This book was published on Ngunnawal country. The publisher would like to acknowledge the people who have told their stories here for countless generations.

For Claire (Year 10/2020). Thanks for letting me borrow your name <3

MINT GROWS EVEN IN THE DARK

Claire knew where the people reported in the news as 'missing under suspicious circumstances' were going. And, if there'd been any justice in the world, she'd have gone to the authorities and reported it.

Sadly, in this instance, said authorities would have investigated her claims and either a) not come out of the little overgrown cave that had opened up at the end of a quiet cul-de-sac in a quiet, overgrown neighbourhood or b) not found anything at all.

Assuming they didn't c) find a bunch of dead bodies and d) blame her.

No. There was no justice in the world, and so Claire could not let anyone know where the wandering missing people had gone, and this annoyed her—on many levels.

Right now, as she stood in the kitchen furiously plucking creased mint leaves from stems woody and long as her forearm, the level it was annoying her on was the level that reminded her there were things in the world that she could not control.

Claire prided herself on control; made a living from it, even, in point of fact. That was the purpose of the tea garden out back, with its neatly ordered rows of tidily clipped herb bushes in all shades of green, in pots black as Hades itself. She'd never be a true Seer like her grandmother, but she was good enough for daily use and what she *did* see, with aid of her various pots and potions, was enough to gain the upper edge most times over fate. Or Fate, depending.

Not that it did anything about the constant stream of disparagement from bloody Alistair, boyfriend of Kirsty, her roommate, himself practically a roommate these days—and not an entirely unwelcome one, he was generous with his contribution to the daily household minutiae, and to the rent—but the snobbery over her 'girl-stuff' i.e. tea leaves and kettles and teacups and brewing (because heaven knew *only* women drank tea, *of* bloody *course*), *that* she could have lived without.

Claire sighed heavily, the green, sharp scent of the mint twining about her like a cat.

There was no justice in the world, and so she was going to have to do something about the missing people herself. The teas had been crystal clear —metaphorically, of course—on that.

She threw the handful of mint leaves into a large stoneware teapot shaped like a turtle, along with a good helping of lavender and ginkgo and furry grey sage. It only took a couple of minutes for the kettle to boil, then she poured herself a small black cup of the resulting tea and waited impatiently for it to cool. Steam twirled and danced and twined upward, and all the while Claire pressed her lips together and drummed her fingernails on the counter. Against the dark grey tile of the kitchen splashback, the steam was clearly visible, pale and ghostly. Twirl, twist. Twist, twine. Spin. Stretch.

The steam yawned like the mouth of a cave.

Stretched into a shape remarkably like a crack.

Became a tangle of roots and weeds.

Lips pursed even tighter, Claire waved the steam away and took up the handle-less teacup. She already knew she needed to visit the cave if she wanted answers, and she hoped the tea would have something less repetitive to share with her.

She slurped at it, hesitant at first, wincing as it almost burnt the tip of her tongue.

Usually, she wouldn't dare a slosh of cold water from the tap—too easy to disrupt the workings, alter the flow, change the vision—but despite her wish for news less repetitive, really, she was only here for confirmation.

So Claire let the tap slop in some cold water and gulped down the sweet-savoury, lightly floral, sharp-tasting tea, swirling counter-clockwise after every third mouthful.

With only half an inch of tea left in the black cup, she set it back on its matching saucer, waited for a slow count of seven, then threw the last of the liquid into the sink.

It wasn't quite the traditional way of doing things, but it was how her grandmother had done it, and if it was good enough for Nana, it was good enough for her.

Droplets coalesced, sparkling on the silver of the sink, over-bright given the cloudy skies outside.

Images formed and shifted as the droplets and small puddles slowly drained. The cave again. A woman's face, crying. A fruit tree. A man, also crying, though somehow managing to look furious at the same time, a moderately thick beard paradoxically narrowing his chin until it almost looked elfin, childlike.

Claire exhaled heavily and rubbed at her forehead. The man was new, and the sense of fury was strong enough that Claire could feel it grabbing at her chest. Interesting.

Briefly, she toyed with the idea of pouring a second cup. Would it add anything? Shed any further clarity on the man, who was—apparently, her sixth sense told her—crying for the woman, or the woman who was crying for reasons as yet unknown?

Or was she just looking for a delay now, when she'd known all along where this would lead?

Claire sighed again, ran the tap to clear the sink, and stalked out of the kitchen, tugging absently at a lock of dark hair.

At the front door—a vibrant shade Claire couldn't decide her feelings on; was it sunshine gold or sulphurous yellow?—she paused as Kirsty called down from upstairs.

"Are you heading to the shops?"

"No," Claire called back, eyebrows quirking at the muffled thumps. Alistair wasn't home; what on earth was Kirsty doing? "Just going for a walk."

Thump.

Thud, thud-bump.

Rearranging furniture, or failing at kick-boxing?

"You okay?" Claire called, just in case.

"Yeah I'm good!"

Claire shrugged one shoulder, realised Kirsty couldn't see her anyway, and let her shoulder drop. "I'm not taking my phone," she called as she opened the front door with its customary squeak. "If you need something... I don't know, shout loud." She glanced up the street, past the five intervening townhouses to the sprawling tangle of green at the end of the cul-de-sac. "I'll hear you."

"Have fun!"

Claire pulled the door shut—slammed it shut, actually, the damn thing had leaked like a sieve when they'd moved in and in resealing it, the bloody tradesman had made it so if you *didn't* slam it, it wouldn't latch closed—though to be fair it didn't leak any more—and headed down the street.

It would have been easy to study the houses she passed as she walked—all skinny, double-storey things jammed elbow to elbow, yellow-and-grey facades disconcertingly commercial, wispy liquid ambers out the front doing a poor job of making the street look like a richer place than it was—or else fix her eyes on the tangle of wilderness ahead, a toothless gap in the block of houses, green swishy grass to her knees presently going to seed and narrow-leafed vines curling sinuous up black-trunked eucalypts, yellow dandelions and white star jasmine and tiny, baby-pink somethings in the weeds.

What was significantly more difficult was to walk casually, normally, splitting her attention between that gap in the houses that seemed to beckon, and the rest of the quiet, empty street.

The windows always seemed to be watching here, even though almost every one of them had its blind drawn.

Claire drew her shoulders back, trying to quiet the itch between her shoulder blades.

A tiny movement: the beige curtain in that window, there, the top floor of the house to her right—it had moved.

Claire paused on the path, squinting at the window. Her stomach twisted, though why she had no idea, it was only a window, only a movement, nothing *fateful* about that.

The curtain twitched aside.

Three women of age indeterminate peered out. Were they old? Young? There must be odd reflections interfering with her view from here, because somehow they seemed to be both.

And they were staring at her.

Claire abruptly realised she was staring at them too. She shot them a glare, then whirled and stomped away, refusing to look back, even though that itch between her shoulder blades was so bad it felt like someone moments away from touching her.

At the end of the cul-de-sac—far enough that Claire couldn't see if the women were still peering at her or not—Claire stopped. The air smelled fresher here, less of the city concrete and more of dirt and damp and growing things. The knee-high grass, bright emerald, swished a little in the wind, a whisper Claire almost felt she understood.

It wasn't a disconcerting feeling; despite being a little frustrating, like catching something important just on the edge of hearing, or knowing you'd just forgotten something significant, it was mostly a pleasant sensation.

She stooped almost idly, snapping the sunny dandelions and pink-and-white clover heads and the bullrush-like tips off the plantain. A pretty bouquet, somehow more colourful than usual under the overcast sky. She could feel the call tugging at her, quiet, insistent, insidious like the cold of a sharp winter's morning. But she'd be darned if she'd go in to it on *its* terms.

So she lingered in the cool of the grass as the sun began to sink behind its curtain of grey clouds, the air slowly dimming as she leaned against a smooth grey gum tree and tilted her head back to look up through the canopy.

She stood so still that a blackbird landed on a small boulder not two paces away, tilting its little black head, eyeing her curiously with its yellow-ringed eye.

Claire smiled—and the bird flitted away, though not too far: it landed on the tussocky grass that grew over the hillock that was the mouth of the cave.

She sighed. *Yes, yes, alright.* Pushed away from the tree that had been holding her up. Rearranged the flowers in slightly sweaty palms.

And headed for the cave.

The entrance was barely noticeable to a casual passerby, nothing more than a narrow crack in between two granite boulders right behind the black trunk of a huge granddaddy eucalypt, the whole lot covered in sod. Claire had to wriggle between tree and rock, a tight squeeze that left one forearm lightly grazed, then twist sideways and bend almost double, leading with her feet and her hips as she clung to the rough, black-barked tree for support.

If the tea was wrong about this passage…

She clenched her jaw, pushed off from the trunk, shimmied through the narrow slice of space between the boulders… and found herself in a rough-hewn tunnel tall enough to stand in and then some.

Her eyebrows tightened. The boulders were tall, but—she reached up, just barely brushing the rough, cold surface of the tunnel's ceiling with her fingertips—not that tall.

"Bigger on the inside," she murmured, and goosebumps rose on her arms. She rubbed them away with the back of her wrist, breathing in the damp, cool, mineral smell of the dirt and rock. The taste was refreshing, in a strange sort of way.

The air cooled; the light dimmed. But right in the liminal space between light and dark, just where the muted sunlight faded out entirely and she lost her footsteps in the black, she spotted a fiery torchlight not too far ahead. It flickered, orange and warm in the darkness.

Heart trilling, rolling her weedy little bouquet in one sweaty palm, Claire headed for the light.

As she drew near, a shadow on the ground shifted—and raised its head, and Claire realised that the underground scent had grown mustier, *furrier*: it was a huge black dog curled up on the floor.

Only it was... two dogs? Perhaps? Three?

She squinted in the flickering light of the torch, hesitated for a second as the closest dog lifted its head and sniffed, nostrils quivering.

Claire batted away the wisp of nervousness that rose in her; far better to be cool, calm and confident, since the dogs could smell what she was feeling.

She took a purposeful, grounding breath and remembered the tea. She, like all other human beings, was fated to die—but it was not this day.

She stepped forward. The dogs—dog? There seemed too few tails and legs for the number of heads—rose to greet her, mouths open in panting smiles, and she bent to run her hands over silken ears and scratch bony stops and tickle her fingers under the chins of smiling probable-Rottweilers.

She smiled back. "Yes yes," she said. "You're all very good dogs."

A last pat on the head for each, and then she moved on, helping herself to the flaming torch from the wall that sputtered and flickered, but seemed otherwise steady enough. It smelled faintly of burning kerosene, and she wondered if that's because it *was* burning kerosene, or if it was only because she expected it to smell that way.

The walk seemed like a dream, both long and short all at once, the kind of dream where at one moment Claire was walking down a rough-hewn passageway in the dark underground, and had always been walking down it, forever, her entire life—and the next she was spilling out into a brightly-lit room that lay somewhere between an old-fashioned library, with floor-to-ceiling bookcases and green, leather-bound volumes lining the shelves, and a very contemporary office, complete with fancy sit-to-stand office desk bearing what seemed very much to be the absolute cutting edge of computing technology.

Claire blinked rapidly.

Footsteps sounded from a corridor that led off to her left, looking for all the world like it could have been a corridor in a modern office building, except that as it hit the middle distance everything seemed to grow kind of fuzzy, like when she put her auntie's glasses on—or like the corridor was only an illusion, covering the darkness that truly lingered there.

A man appeared.

No.

The man appeared, the one the tea had shown her, his skin a little darker than she'd expected—a very medium brown, darker than her dark olive—and Claire was startled to realise that he wasn't in fact, crying, because not only had the tea shown that to her, but the energy emanating from him was sorrow so deep and so thick she could hardly breathe.

It took everything she had not to rush to him, to run her thumb over his wild eyebrows to smooth them, to comfort him—and as he realised she was there, their eyes meeting for the fractionest of an instant, he seemed to want the comfort.

It was the kind of sensation she was tempted to write off to imagination, however, since the second he processed the fact of her existence his entire demeanour changed, becoming brusque and businesslike. "If you'll please take a... seat." He cocked his head, frowning, eyebrows drawn low and tight over dark, intelligent eyes. "What are you doing here? You're not scheduled to be dead."

Claire blinked. "Not yet, anyway." She didn't have to add 'I hope'; Seeing was a blessing and a curse, and it birthed knowledge that was both blessing and curse, but at the same time, Claire had always taken a lot of comfort from the fact that the time of her death *was* scheduled. It certainly put one's calendar in perspective, knowing one had a very *specifically* finite time in which to get things done. She shifted the weedy bouquet.

"Then how are you here?" His puzzled frown charmed her, in a way: it was a difficult puzzle she could easily solve, and those were her favourite. "Never mind," he said, dismissing his own question with a shake of his head. "I don't have time for—I don't have time."

For a brief moment, the deep anguish gripped him again, and his shoulders slumped, and his face slackened, and his eyes pressed closed as though that could hold him together. "I apologise for my lack of hospitality."

He whistled sharply.

Claire jumped.

"Allow me at least to procure you a guide." He opened his eyes again, like a curtain lifting sorrow forcibly aside, and he smiled kindly at her. "Please —well, I was going to say don't be alarmed by the dog, but you must have met him on the way in, so." He shrugged, disarmed.

Footsteps echoed down the passageway Claire had come through, toenails clacking on stone.

The big black dog flung itself into the light—and Claire recoiled for just the briefest of seconds as she noted that she had, in fact, been correct, and there were too many heads for legs-and-tails, and the dog was apparently Cerberus, or maybe Spot.

She glanced sidelong at the man—Hades?—as the dog threw itself at her, all three tongues trying to lick her to death at once.

The dog slobber cut through all her other emotions, as dog slobber is wont to do.

Claire giggled. Pushed the dog down.

Smoothed out her skirt in some attempt to reclaim her dignity.

Gave in and knelt on the floor while all three heads of the dog writhed in happiness around her. Weedy flowers fell to the ground as she abandoned them in favour of happy dog fur.

"Follow him out," probable-Hades said with a gentle, one-sided smile—the kind of smile pet owners everywhere adopted at the sight of someone else appreciating their pet. "He'll keep you safe."

Claire rolled her eyes. "I don't need to be kept safe."

"No," Hades said musingly. "I don't suppose you do." He turned to retreat down the corridor.

"Wait!" Claire flung herself to her feet, trying to push Cerberus away long enough for her to actually rearrange her skirt. "I need to see you!"

Hades turned back to her, one eyebrow lifted under his thick, dark, densely curled hair. "You've seen me," he said. "I have places to be." He sketched a quick bow.

"But the missing people!" she said. "You need to let them go!"

He hesitated, one hand on the door frame, mouth open as though to speak—

And then he shook his head, the aura of sorrow rising again. "I have places I need to be."

Claire stood watching his retreating back for a moment, then folded her arms tightly over her chest and pursed her lips. "Well."

Beside her, Cerberus rolled onto his back, exposing a generous expanse of stomach just begging to be scratched.

Absently, Claire rubbed it with one foot, arms still folded, brows still furrowed. It was no good him telling her he had places to be; the missing *people* had places to be, and those places weren't *here*, in the Underworld-apparent. Maybe once, in ancient times, this was how things had been done—she made a whole raft of mental sticky notes with questions to ask Grandmother next time her spirit came calling—but this was *not* how things were done *today*. Not here. Not in this part of the world.

Not in *Claire's* part of the world.

There was such a thing as closure for the families, after all.

There, she was decided then.

With a quick glance at the lefthand passage that was more furtive than she'd have liked, Claire strode straight ahead across the library-office, slipping behind the desk to an unobtrusive wooden door that practically shouted 'staff only'.

Cerberus fish-flopped himself upright, toenails tick-tacking on the polished floorboards as he followed her, nostrils quivering.

"Hush," Claire told him. "I'm just going to take a peek, okay?"

She slipped through the door, latching it quietly behind herself.

She was somewhere dark. Somewhere large, and empty, and echoey—and apparently not quite constrained by the usual rules of time and space, because Cerberus appeared in front of her, the two outer heads panting with lolling tongues while the middle squinted suspiciously at her.

She checked the door behind her. Still latched. Hmm.

Footsteps (sans toenails) echoed in the darkness and for a moment, Claire, tensed, adrenalin kicking her heart-beat into overdrive. She pressed her back against the door, gripping the doorknob behind her. Stay? Go?

Dim light appeared in the middle distance that quickly resolved into an elderly woman with glasses, silvery hair and a sleeveless, softly draping plum-purple dress, carrying a lantern.

Let her speak first, Claire decided. Then she could come up with a suitable excuse, if she needed one.

Other people loved to fill silences, and one could learn a lot about them while they did.

Sadly, it seemed the woman had studied at the same school of humanity Claire had: she came to a halt next to Cerberus, one hand drifting idly down to rub his ears, and stood frowning deeply at Claire as though *she* were the puzzle.

Claire sniffed quietly.

Seconds ticked by.

Cerberus sat abruptly and scratched wildly at his middle-left ear, groaning as he did.

He stood. Shook vigorously. All three heads turned to the elderly woman, panting with three happy, open-mouthed smiles.

The woman sighed. "Well alright then," she said. "If you insist."

Claire was fairly sure she was talking to the dog, but her gaze never left Claire's—and Claire, despite her resolve, shivered.

"Come on then," the woman said, turning and walking away.

Was she supposed to follow?

"Do you want something to drink or not?" The woman threw over her shoulder. "No?" she said when Claire didn't move. "What about answers?"

Claire let go of the door handle.

"Ah," said the woman shrewdly. "Indeed." She waited a moment while Claire caught up, the darkness closing gently in around them beyond the boundary of the lantern.

It smelled… fruity.

Not something Claire would have expected here in—

"You know where you are then, I suppose," the woman said, marching forward with purposeful strides that belied her apparent age.

Claire nodded, realised the woman was unlikely to have seen given she was half a step ahead, and cleared her throat. "Yes. I assume. This is Cerberus," she said as the big black-and-tan dog triple-nudged his way in between them.

"This hairy lump," the woman said with a dismissive glance at the beast—but then, although she resumed her straight-backed, straight-gazed walk, she let the hand not holding the lantern dangle down and ruffle a furry black ear. "Left," she said, and without further warning turned at a right angle.

Claire hastened to keep up—but the woman halted almost immediately, reaching for something Claire presumed must be on a nearby wall.

In front of them, lights came up on a small sitting area: three burgundy curve-backed armchairs huddled around a low wooden coffee table, plain topped, plain legged, but bordered with a carved frieze of… well, Claire couldn't quite make it out in the light.

Which… The darkness was still wrapped cozily around them, and if the woman had flicked a switch somewhere it hadn't been on a wall, or at least not any wall Claire could detect—nor had it been for any specific lights she could see, even if it had increased the strange, ambient lighting.

The woman crossed what Claire could now see as a black-and-white tiled floor—Cerberus's nails clacked on it as he followed, until he got to the thick, plush rug delineating the sitting space—and sat herself down in the closest armchair, setting the lantern onto the table in front of her.

The lantern light lit the carved frieze on the edge of the low table more brightly—and Claire rather wished it hadn't.

"Persephone is dying."

Claire blinked at that, tearing her eyes away from gaping, skeletal mouths and carved, contorted bones. "I thought she was immortal?"

"Was is not is, young lady." The woman peered down her nose at Claire despite the fact that Claire was still standing, and scratched idly at Cerberus's ears as he flumped to the floor beside her chair. The three heads clamoured over each other for her attention.

Three heads, all apparently equally starved of pats.

Claire rolled her eyes just a little, sat herself down in the curved armchair next to the woman instead of the one opposite, and with a dutiful sigh reached out and began stroking the silky black ear closest to her.

Cerberus groaned with happiness.

The woman gave Claire an appraising look. "You could replace her, you know." She tapped her finger firmly on the low wooden table by their knees and a tall carafe of water, condensation glistening on its outside, appeared on a silver tray, accompanied by two plain glasses. "He will love you, with time, and you he."

Claire's eyes widened and she stiffened. "*Excuse me?*" Her heart thumped wildly. Was that a reasoned suggestion, or a prophecy?

...She didn't really want to know.

The woman shrugged. "You heard his grief, did you not. Only someone compatible could do that."

"*Compatible?*" Claire's eyebrows just about reached escape velocity. "Lady, I don't know how it's done where you're from, but where I'm from..."

Her heart hammered in betrayal. Her aunt had been a promise-match, after all.

Cerberus nudged at her hand with his closest head, whining pitifully.

Claire exhaled and resumed his ear scritchies.

"He is grieving, you see," the woman continued, watching Claire appraisingly over her glasses. "She will be gone soon, and he refuses to leave her side for more than a few minutes. Wants to make the most of the time he has left. I can understand that, of course, but it does make the more *bureaucratic* side of things down here rather complicated."

Claire frowned, her brow furrowing. "How so?" The tea hadn't specified that, had just noted that the man—Hades—was grieving, probably over a woman, and that he was in the cave with the missing people. Was he calling people down when he wasn't meant to, when they weren't yet scheduled to die? Or were they simply wandering down here, summoned by a grief they could sense but not understand?

The woman shrugged, the draped folds of her sleeveless plum dress shifting in the light. "He is refusing to leave, and so the souls of the dying are being called to him rather than he to them, and those who might otherwise live find themselves drawn in by his emotions."

Ah. Both, then. Claire's frown deepened. "But he's not the Grim Reaper. He doesn't go out and *collect* souls, that's Thanos."

"Used to be," the woman said. "Times change."

"Belief changes," Claire said slowly. That was the problem with Seeing, the one thing no one warned you about until it was too late: believe in something hard enough and it had a way of manifesting. Belief could change reality—nothing magical about that, people did it all the time, believing in things like love and justice and equity—so if you'd been given a glimpse of a future that was, or even that *might* be... Well. A little bit of knowledge paired with a whole lot of belief could get you killed.

Or believed right out of existence, if Claire was reading between the lines correctly.

"But people adore Persephone," she said. "She can be fading from lack of belief."

The woman smiled wryly. "People adore the *idea* of Persephone. They made her relatable. Human. Mortal. A mortal falling in love with the god of the underworld?" She shrugged. "Fashions change, and apparently right now that's the height of romance, at least in some circles. In enough circles to matter," she added, with particularly pointed eyebrows.

"And here I am," Claire said, aiming for conversational and missing just slightly to the side of acerbic, "another mortal ready to replace the goddess who was believed into mortality, ready to carry on the mantle and continue the romance. Because after all, human to goddess is popular these days too. The commoner gets the prince." Claire pursed her lips and sniffed, loudly this time.

Cerberus looked at her in alarm, all three heads twisting to stare close-mouthed at her.

Claire run a thumb down the stop of the closest one. Its eyes closed in bliss, and the other two heads relaxed.

The woman shrugged. "Or perhaps not. Perhaps you are fine with allowing souls to stray in here willynilly, come what may.

"My being here wouldn't necessarily stop that," Claire pointed out. "Unless you wanted me to physically kick him out the door to go do his job."

Which... Hmm. Was that a thing she could do? She narrowed her eyes again, squinting thoughtfully at the darkness, trying to decide.

She'd done worse, probably, to men potentially more stubborn.

Her finger drummed on the wooden tip of the chair's arm.

Hmm.

This time, the woman laughed. "Olympus help us all, you really might, mightn't you."

Claire's cheeks heated, but she forced herself not to squirm. After all, the light was dim. "Perhaps," she said. "If I decided it was both necessary and within my control."

"Control, yes." The woman closed one eye and seemed to stare through her with the other, though her hands still ran idly over Cerberus's closest head.

"Pomegranates," Claire said abruptly.

"I'm sorry?"

"Pomegranates. That's what the darkness smells like." Claire took a long, deep inhale. Yes. Definitely, absolutely, the warm, soft darkness smelled like pomegranate juice.

"Pomegranates." The woman shook her head, not in disagreement so much as disbelief. But her smile brightened, less wry, more rueful—and then practically genuine. "How's your Ancient Greek?" she asked, and stuck out one creased-and-lined hand. "Themis," she said. "The name's Themis."

Claire blinked, unfamiliar, though she took the proffered hand and shook it politely.

Themis sighed deeply. "Astrea takes care of most of the large-scale issues, but I am still permitted to wield some influence, though goodness knows that's waning too, belief being what it is these days. My daughters get most of the work now, of course."

"Your... daughters?"

"You saw them, I think. On your way here."

Claire's brow wrinkled. "I didn't see..." But she did, didn't she? The three women, clustered in the window behind the beige curtain, the strange reflection making them seem both old and young simultaneously.

Hades, Persephone; the Underworld, and Cerberus...

"The Fates are your daughters?"

Themis nodded, eyes sparkling. "Good girl. You have wits enough. You will do well."

Claire set her cup of water down and scowled. "I haven't said I'll do anything."

"No," Themis said mildly. "But you will consider it. You'd do the job admirably. It'd soften some of your A-type edges, but give you a chance to really stretch your wings. You've always known you were born to run things."

An uncomfortable itch in her spine. Claire lifted her cup and drank deeply to avoid answering. Cold water gulped down her throat steadied her a little.

This was absurd. Ridiculous. None of this could be...

She wanted to say 'real', but that was the point, wasn't it? She was a Seer, she knew and saw and engaged with things all the time that other folks would have scoffed at. She *knew* the world was bigger than it looked, smaller on the outside and utterly, utterly vaster on the inside than anyone could ever imagine.

This was, as they said, her *jam*.

And... Themis was not wrong when she noted that Claire loved to organise things.

She was reasonably adept at bucking Fate, too, which might come in handy in this particular role.

Claire pursed her lips against the smooth, firm rim of the cup. Stared at Themis, who was pretending to ignore her momentarily as she rearranged golden cushions that seemed to have appeared from nowhere behind her back.

Claire set her glass down on the table with a click. "Okay," she said. "What are the terms? Do I have to do the whole winter thing? Four months below ground and all that?"

Themis nodded. "Four months was the minimum, yes. Seph chose to stay longer sometimes, you know. Once she and Hades got to know each other."

Claire pursed her lips and placed that thought aside to deal with later. Maybe she would 'get to know' Hades, maybe she wouldn't. Regardless, she wasn't about to make it the basis of her decision, because that was not how good decisions were made. "And spring? What's the deal with that?"

Themis shrugged. "It will come regardless of what you do, but if you take up this mantle, then you are able to... help."

Claire leaned back in her seat, her back tall and straight. "Elaborate."

"Your presence is an amplifier. You make things more of what they are."

Claire's breath caught in her throat. She opened her mouth, rearranged the ensuing sentence, and said, "You mean now, or if I take up this role?"

Themis shrugged a shoulder, one side of her mouth curving upward beneath bright eyes. "Yes."

Claire was not holding her breath, but the breaths she *was* taking were shallow and thin, her shoulders all bunched up at her neck and her chest high and tight. *After all, isn't that what Seeing is, on a fundamental level? Seeing, believing… amplifying?*

Themis shook her head ruefully. "Child, I know you better than you could think. If you were to have any goddess of my pantheon, it would be me. Your oracles, your prophesies?" She raised her eyebrows pointedly, her head tilting just a little as though the point she was making was obvious.

Which… it was, wasn't it. "Oh," Claire said softly.

Themis: goddess of justice, law, divine order (all of which could be summarised simply as 'control') —and also associated with oracles. Hmm.

Claire's pulse kicked, her mind scrambling through all the possibilities. *I'm an amplifier. I see and I believe.* And this position would capitalise on that ability, give it power beyond anything she'd ever dreamed…

I could amplify anything with this much belief behind me…

So wasn't this, after all, everything she'd ever wanted? Themis was talking about, if not absolute control, then certainly the ability to wield a very hefty rock to change the course of Fate's riparian flow. The ability to See as much as she wanted, to *believe it* as hard as she wanted, to *amplify* it, all with the blessing of a patron if not as powerful as she once was in the Greek pantheon's prime, then still more powerful than anyone in the human world could dream…

Claire's jaw twitched.

Cerberus mouthed at her hand, which had fallen still.

"I'll think about it," she said, staring at the darkness that surrounded them, idly stroking Cerberus's closest head. It wasn't an unfriendly sort of darkness, by any means.

And it had been calling to her.

At this point, it felt sort of familiar.

And she'd always been rather fond of pomegranates.

"Very well," Themis said. "You have until your week's end to make your decision."

Claire looked sharply back at her. "If I decline?"

Themis shrugged, a full-bodied gesture of resignation this time. "Then the search continues. One way or another, a replacement must be found. Belief demands it." She set her glass down on the table and stared off into the darkness through her glasses. "Can't have all these souls turning up unannounced," she muttered. "Quite untenable. Quite."

THEY WERE IN THE KITCHEN, MAKING DINNER, MOVING NOT together but at least in complementary orbits as they prepared their respective meals.

"I might move out," Claire said casually as Kirsty dodged her neatly with the butter dish.

Kirsty plopped the dish down on the draining board by the sink. "Oh?"

Claire shrugged to the open fridge, cool air wafting against her cheeks. "Just a thought."

"Well, just a thought," Kirsty said over her shoulder as she slapped toast onto a plain white ceramic plate, "but in the nicest possible sense, I wouldn't mind a bit."

"Well, I won't do it right away," Claire added, reaching for the half-empty jar of tomato paste on the top shelf. Her pulse kicked. "A few months, maybe. By next winter, for sure," she continued, closing the fridge with a soft little whumph.

Kirsty narrowed her eyes, her gaze burning into Claire's peripheral vision, butterknife poised in the air. "That's not like you. You're not a 'go with the flow' kind of person. What's really going on?"

Claire sighed deeply. "I... got a job offer," she said carefully. The label on the tomato paste had wrinkled in one corner, dog-earred.

At least Cerberus liked her.

She'd always wanted a dog.

"Really?" Kirsty said. "Doing what?"

"Change management," Claire said glibly, but it was a public service town and Kirsty took it without so much as a blink.

"Sure," Kirsty said, scraping the butterknife over her toast with that distinctive scraping sound. "I can see that."

"Really?" Claire's eyebrow rose of their own accord. She put them down where they belonged, and the tomato paste down on the bench.

"Sure." Kirsty shrugged again. "Tea?" She'd finished spreading the butter and was already filling the kettle, the faucet protesting loudly as it did sometimes when it was in a mood.

"Mine won't..." Claire side-eyed the pan on the stove with vegetables bubbling away, the pot of rice steaming gently behind it, and sighed. Her dinner wouldn't be ready for another fifteen minutes or so, but that was plenty of time for a cup of tea in the meantime. "Sure," she said. "Fine. Just let me add the tomato paste."

She did, and by that time the kettle had boiled and Kirsty was slopping the water into two stoneware mugs and throwing in helping handfuls of the mint Claire had harvested earlier in the week.

Mint.

Claire was going to miss growing mint.

She accepted the mug from Kirsty, who took her own and her plate of plain buttered toast around the other side of the bench, where she perched on one of the black barstools, watching as Claire pottered in the kitchen.

Still. Mint grew everywhere, right? It was resilient and adaptable, and surely she could take some of that with her, maybe keep it alive? She sipped at the burningly hot liquid, sharp and fresh.

Persephone had had flowers with her, after all… She cradled the mug in both hands, the heat seeping into her fingers.

Start with mint. See if it lived. Then stretch for more after that. Perhaps by winter she'd have a little tea garden going after all.

Claire startled. By winter?

Carefully, she set the mug down on the bench. She was fairly sure she'd decided to take the job, but since when had she decided the timing? Hoping to have a tea garden going by winter meant planting things out roughly, well, *now*…

"What's up?" Kirsty said around a mouthful of toast, crumbs framing her mouth, her light eyes creased in kindly-meant puzzlement. "You've been weird all week."

Claire shook her head. "It's just this job," she said, then turned her back on Kirsty to stir her concoction on the stove. Savoury smells of tomato paste and spicy lime seasoning wafted up to greet her. They wound about her like steam from a teacup, yawning and stretching, cavernous.

Claire dispelled them with a wave of her hand and scowled. The whole point of Seeing was to be able to *defy* Fate, not to be pushed into it.

Back to the circular problem at the heart of it though, where Seeing became believing became reality. She'd caught a glimpse of the future Themis was offering; if she believed in it too hard, it would be real.

Which was fine... so long as she was sure she actually wanted it.

"If you had an opportunity," she said slowly, still with her back to Kirsty, "that would give you a... a really good job in a position of respect and authority, and it... kind of sounded like it was at least very well suited for you, if not exactly *made* for you..."

Kirsty had gone still at the bench; all sounds of toast consumption had ceased.

Claire tried to breathe out the tension knotting her shoulders and chest. It failed.

She stirred the pan some more.

The steam waved at her.

"*What*?" Kirsty said. "You can't leave me hanging like that. If all that, then *what*?"

Claire shrugged against the tension. "I don't know. What would you be willing to risk for it?"

Kirsty narrowed her eyes in Claire's peripheral vision. "Claire, you are making this sound dodgy as hell. Who's offering you the job, and what are they asking you to risk?"

Claire shrugged again. "Nothing, I just have to… move. Be out of town for at least four months of the year is all. To, uh, be on the ground of the organisation, that sort of thing."

"And they're letting you work remotely the other eight months of the year?"

"Uh, yeah. I guess?"

Kirsty's demeanour shifted, a grin cleaving her concern. "Dude. Eight months remote work? Sounds like a dream job to me!"

"Oh." Something fluttered in Claire's chest. "But, I mean, it's going to be hard to find somewhere that will let me rent just eight months of the year, right? The job doesn't pay well enough that I can afford double rent a third of the year." Technically, the job didn't pay at all, although with all the powers of belief… Claire shrugged at the itch in her shoulder blades. One had to be practical in all matters, and that was what she was being: practical.

Kirsty shrugged. "If the job's that good, it'll work out."

This time it was a twist, not a flutter. "But how do you *know* that?" Kirsty wasn't a Seer, didn't know what it was Claire really did—and yet, she did seem to fumble on through her own life relatively fine.

"I don't. I just… believe it." Kirsty made a sort of 'what can you do' gesture with one hand, her mouth quirking to one side before she reclaimed the last of her toast from the white plate. She bit into it with a loud crunch. "Sometime you just gotta have faith, Claire," she said around a mouthful of crumbs.

The pan bubbled enthusiastically, tomato and lime and spice and steam.

Claire scowled at it.

Just believe it.

Heh.

The irony.

ANOTHER WEEK HAD PASSED. THE FULL MOON HAD COME and gone, and Claire had just about given up drinking tea because every damn cup wanted to tell her the same damn thing: she was going, she was going soon, she was leaving well before winter and accepting the job.

"I *know*," she told the current puddle of tea gleaming at her from the bottom of the sink before she swished a finger through it, turned the tap on, washed it away. *I know. I just wish it felt more like my choice and less like something I'd Seen.*

She *could* deny it, of course. She'd fought Fate before and won—or the Fates, she supposed, now.

But…

In her mind's eye, Themis peered over her glasses at Claire, one hand resting on Cerberus's head.

And Hades stared at her, startlement opening his face but also something more—something… intrigued.

Claire scowled, shut the tap off, and grabbed a tea towel to dry her hands.

The problem was, of course, that she didn't exactly *want* to defy Fate this time. The missing people were still missing, with more joining them every couple of days, and the police were baffled, and it was becoming a political to-do, and the families—of course—were distraught.

She was still the only person who could do something about it.

She still resented being told to do the thing she'd been planning to do regardless.

Well, fine then. If the thing had to be done, then best to do it and get it done. And she had to tell Themis her decision anyway.

She brushed at her long wine-red skirt even though her hands were now dry, straightened her shoulders—and picked up the little pot of mint that grew on the kitchen windowsill. What else to take?

Well. She wasn't going to *stay* right now. Not necessarily. Not without saying goodbye to Kirsty.

…Claire sighed, tucked the mint under her

shoulder, and headed for the front door.

Alistair came pounding down the steep, narrow stairs of the house. "Sup," he said. And then, because he loved to be the bearer of any news, good or bad, "Did you hear three more people went missing just overnight?"

Claire sighed. That was in addition to the two yesterday, and one the day before that. "Yes," and she didn't mean to clip the word quite as harshly as she did. "I heard."

Nearly a baker's dozen, now. She sighed again.

"Terrible, isn't it." Alastair's tone conveyed no sense of sorrow or regret whatsoever. At the bottom of the stairs he peered, suddenly suspicious, at her mint pot. "Casually taking your plants for walks now?"

Claire stared evenly at him. "Yes."

Let him think what he wanted. She'd learned long ago not to care about *that* particular thing she couldn't control.

He blinked, a little taken aback. "Oh. Well. Have fun then, I guess."

"I will."

She yanked the something-yellow door open, slammed it behind her, and absolutely did not stalk down the street.

A couple of houses down, she glanced back—not to say farewell to the house, she was coming back, she absolutely was, she hadn't packed clothes, or toiletries, or anything apart from mint

—and started in surprise. Herbs, springing up in her footsteps from the cracks in the pavement—mint, mostly, but she spotted a sprig of something that was either parsley or coriander too, and the fuzzy little nose of sage budding through there to the right.

Oh, she thought. *It begins.*

Well. Herbs were more practical for her than flowers, she supposed. *It'll make planting a tea garden easy.*

She sniffed in passing amusement.

Down the street, through air that had a distinct touch of autumn to now (though seasonal change was not *quite* here, according to the calendar), a gentle breeze caressing her face and ruffling her dark hair. She picked a strand of it out of her mouth.

Would the missing people be sent back sooner rather than later?

Her chest constricted as she realised that was one thing that really *was* in her control.

End of the street.

Into the weeds.

Squish between the huge grey-and-white eucalypt and the grassy boulders, into the crack that led to the cave that led to the passage and on to her destiny.

Ahead of her, a small knot of ghostly shapes shone in the darkness.

That was a lot more than three.

Six, seven... at least eight that she could see

from here, possibly more, though it was hard to tell with them all bunching together and shifting and ebbing in the dim light, themselves no more than translucent, pearly shades.

Well this was never going to do.

Claire's hands knotted at her sides and she set her jaw as she set out down the stony corridor.

The stories neglected to mention how resentful it was possible to feel once one had discovered one's destiny—not because the destiny itself was horrible, but because the mere fact of having a destiny meant one was not in control of it.

She'd fought Fate before and won.

She'd fought Fate before.

...She'd fought.

For control over her own life, yes, but for other people, for the ones who didn't have agency, or couldn't exert it, or who'd had it stripped away.

People like the ones now drifting along in front of her.

Claire's heavy sigh filled her mouth with the taste of damp minerals and stone—the air was warmer, somehow, than it should have been.

She emerged into the office-cum-library, where the pearly shades were drifting around aimlessly, like smoke, or fog, or oblivion.

Across the room, Cerberus lifted his head from the black rug—he could have been a pile of rug himself until he moved—flared his nostrils once or twice as he checked her over, and then grinned with all three heads.

"At least someone's happy to see me," Claire muttered.

Well. That wasn't exactly right. It wasn't that no one wanted her here—quite the opposite, Themis at least was practically *keen* to have her.

Claire took a deep, steadying breath of bookish air. *Right*, she told herself. *See those people there? You are doing this for them. Because you believe it's the right thing to do. And we all know what belief does, so quit acting like a baby and get on with it.*

She nodded, firmly, entirely to herself, but Cerberus scrambled to his feet and ambled over as though he'd heard her declaration and had decided he'd better chaperone her after all.

She crossed the room. Opened the door behind the desk. "Themis?" she called into the darkness. "I've made my decision."

"And what is that?" Themis seemed to materialise out of the darkness, the same plum-purple, draping dress on as last time, the same wire-rimmed glasses, the same lantern in her hand.

"I'm the only one who knows where the missing souls are, the ones who are here too early. I want them sent back home." She held herself motionless, barely breathing.

Themis nodded. "You'll have to take it up with him, of course."

"Then let me talk to him now." Closure was closure, whether now or in three months' time... But she couldn't think of a single good reason to make the families wait, not when it was within her abilities now to avoid that.

Themis peered over her glasses at Claire. "So you will accept the deal?"

Claire lifted her chin. "Yes."

A nod, the lantern in Themis's hand bobbing. "I will arrange for your Seeing to be blessed."

"No."

Why was Claire's heart suddenly pounding? She'd made this part of the decision days ago, right after her talk with Kirsty. So why did this suddenly feel like an epiphany?

"No?" Themis tilted her head, peering at Claire with narrowed eyes, through her glasses this time. She raised the lantern so its light fell squarely on Claire's face. "No," she repeated softly. "Well. This is a turn." A smile spread over her face that quickly turned into a grin. "It takes a strong woman indeed to recognise that there are things in this world that she cannot control and not let that diminish her courage one bit. Yes," she added, "yes I think the world will have well of you. Come," she said, and beckoned Claire away from the safety of the door.

Cerberus wagged his tail, thump-thump-thumping against Claire's thigh.

A deep breath. A resnugging of the mint pot under her arm.

Claire followed the lantern light into the darkness, not knowing what to expect—the tea hadn't shown the way forward after this.

She thought of Kirsty, grinning at the kitchen bench. *I just... believe.*

The note Claire had written that same night, explaining that she'd be back in a couple of months, in spring, and that Kirsty was welcome to shove her stuff into storage and charge her for it when she got back, rent out her room, that sort of thing.

She hadn't intended to stay today, quite honestly. She'd just wanted to be prepared.

You know. In case.

...She was utterly unprepared.

...She was going to do it anyway. Whatever it took to send those missing people home—and fulfil her destiny.

Claire took a deep, long breath of air that smelled of pomegranates and mint, rested her free hand on Cerberus's head, followed as Themis took her on a long and winding path through darkness that was warm and quiet and familiar.

Anyway. It was still summer, if only just. Three-plus months was time enough to learn what would be expected of her before she *had* to stay. Didn't they always say it took three months to learn a new job?

For a moment she was back in her kitchen, hearing for the first time of the missing people, seeing for the first time the yawning cave in the puddle of tea in her kitchen sink.

For a moment, then, she'd thought there was no justice left in world.

Now, she knew there was—so long as there was someone to believe in it.

Besides. Three months was plenty long enough
to learn how to grow mint in the dark.

# ABOUT THE AUTHOR

AMY LAURENS is an Australian author of fantasy and science fiction for all ages. Her fantasy novella *Bones Of The Sea*, about creepy magical bones and carnivorous mist, won the 2021 Aurealis Award for Best Fantasy Novella.

Amy has also written the award-winning portal-fantasy *Sanctuary* series about Edge, a 13-year-old girl forced to move to a small country town because of witness protection (the first book is *Where Shadows Rise*), the humorous fantasy *Kaditeos* series, following newly graduated Evil Overlord Mercury as she attempts to acquire a castle, the young adult series *Storm Foxes*, about love and magic and family in small town Australia, and a whole host of shorter works.

Amy also writes non-fiction books, often on various aspects of writing. Also dogs. Lots of dogs.

You can find out more about her at
www.AmyLaurens.com

READ MORE BY AMY LAURENS!

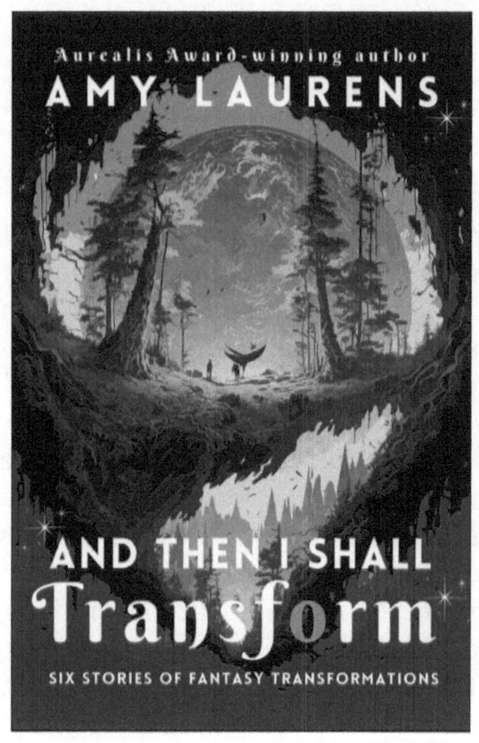

Six fantasy short stories
available in print and ebook
from InkprintPress.com
and all major online retailers

AND THEN I SHALL TRANSFORM

In Which Leaves Are
Common Sense

Most people think leaves fall in autumn because they die, fluttering drifts of red and yellow and orange and brown, twirling on a breeze that smells like the promise of ice before falling to skitter along the ground with a hollow tick-tick-tick.

Most people, it turns out, are wrong.

About many things of course, but in this case about the leaves: deciduous trees don't just shed their leaves wantonly, carelessly—or even regretfully.

No.

Deciduous trees lose their leaves because they are frugal.

Turns out, the only reason the leaves change colour in the first place—be that ruby or pumpkin, butternut or hazel, or some striated rainbow in between—is because the cooling weather lulls the plant into sleepiness, and a sleeping plant is a plant that can't eat (frozen leaves aren't much good at collecting sunlight anyway, not when frost bursts their cell walls like bubbles, sharp fragments of ice severing pathways like a knife through warm, fresh neurons).

The colour change is just the outward signal of the tree's common sense: drawing back in all the nutrients the leaf has to offer, slurping them back into the trunk where the tree can nurse on them all winter long, shedding the now-empty leaves like scales, sloughing them off like old skin, discarding dead storage units until the risk of frostbite has passed.

The day I realised I could do the same changed my life.

The snow was—predictably—cold. It was also early, and I'd been caught out hiking unprepared, which was just about the dumbest thing I'd managed to do yet in my life—apart from, maybe, George, and also attending New Beat University. An avid hiker since I'd been old enough to carry any sort of day pack with my parents, I knew the risks inside and out, backward and forward, up-side and down.

Never go hiking alone.

Always pack extra Puritabs.

Let people know where you're going, and when you expect to be back.

Take warmer things than you think you'll need.

No one gives advice on what to do when your hike-mate has a sudden attack of lunar-cy, though, three days before the full moon. No one tells you what to do when you're abruptly alone in a sea of grey-trunked eucalypt trees and tea tree scrub that stinks like face cleanser and scratches like the blazes, and you've now got two packs' worth of gear to hike out. Alone.

Werewolves are not considerate hiking buddies, let me be the first to assure you.

Well. Amendment: Probably some of them are, maybe even most of them.

George? Not so much.

(In hindsight, unsurprising: he'd never been a very considerate roommate, either, no matter what physical form he was in.)

And, of course, it was cold.

And as I stood in the clearing where considerate wildlife had trampled down the tussock grass and a fallen gum tree was busy turning silver as it weathered, cold air singeing the inside of my nostrils and burning the tip of my nose, I realised I had a choice: I could get really, *really* cold as I sat around waiting for George to human up again—probably in three or four days once the moon had passed, but then again, he wasn't supposed to have wolfed out this early either, so who knew?—or I could get really really *warm* trying to hike two packs' worth of gear back out.

Or—I scratched my nose, face screwed up—I

could redistribute the gear, take the expensive or vital stuff out in one pack, leave the rest somewhere covered and come back when it was safe.

With someone other than George, of course.

Bloody George.

I sighed heavily, rolled my pack over onto its back like a floundering sea lion, and began unbuckling the straps. Stupid to think I could hike a whole day out with both full packs. Not worth the risk.

The sky told me what it thought of that: the clouds that had been fitfully scudding across the sky coagulated into something thick and soupy and so low it seemed like I could practically touch it (or at least throw something high enough to touch it, like a rock, or maybe George, who deserved to be tossed into the sky) and the sky began to spit at me.

I rolled my eyes at the melodrama, rustled the brim of my cherry-red raincoat down over my forehead, and set about repacking the packs.

Out came my bag of dirty clothes. Would I regret leaving them if I needed extra warmth? Probably not.

Stupid weather, sky-spit freezing my fingers and making them slow.

Sleeping mat. Ditched. I had one night max to spend outdoors, and that was if I spent the rest of today lollygagging around instead of moving at pace.

Stupid moon, exerting whatever stupid influence it was over stupid werewolves at a stupid time of the month.

Sleeping bag.

Well. Obviously I was going to hold onto that one, just in case.

Only one though. George could keep his own furry butt warm if it came to that.

Food—check, definitely coming with. Compass, maps, cook stove—yes, yes and yes.

Tent. Obviously. Just in case.

Dammit. I'd have to take both halves.

I fished the fly and poles out of George's pack and rammed them into my own.

The sky stopped spitting, and started snowing at me, frigid air turning my fingers red, the scent of the bush subtly shifting from eucalypt to wet grass and now to snow itself.

The hell.

It was March. Yes, okay, fine, it was autumn by the calendar, but the last five, ten years March had grown *hot*. Like, summer hot. No one reasonably expected even a sudden transient fit of cold weather until April, which was why I'd agreed to this hike with George in the first place.

A cold snap? Sure. Unfortunate, but this wasn't our first hike in the bush and we'd brought layers. Snow?

What. The actual. Hell.

I scowled at the steely clouds, shoved the last of the necessities into my pack, and drew the drawstring tight around its neck.

Flipped the lid of the pack shut, canvas scuffing loudly in the silence of the bush. Snapped the buckles shut—snap, snap, echoing around the clearing.

A third snap.

I froze.

My pack definitely only had two buckles to close, and George's pack was right there in front of me, wallowing on the ground like an unholy grey hippopotamus.

My ears tried to crawl off my head as I tried to surveil the bush around me without appearing to.

...A rustle, perhaps? Behind and to my left, where the gum trees thinned in both density and girth and the spiky, pale tussock grass traced a path down a gentle slope to a green hollow largely occupied by a white cedar of impressive height.

The dang berries on the cedar were toxic. I knew that. George knew that. But did George's lunar form know that?

I may or may not have let my pack fall sideways with a bit of firm assistance as I swore and clambered to my feet.

Definitely a rustle, that now became a susurrus of disturbed grass as something grey and the size of a large kangaroo or a small wolf vanished into the teatree scrub.

I ground my teeth. Inhaled icy-cold air. Buried my hands under my armpits and cursed past-me momentarily for not packing gloves, summer-like weather be damned. Then I trudged after the critter toward the hollow.

The white cedar gleamed like a golden crown amid the grey-and-olive eucalypts, framed above by the grey sky, its buttery autumn leaves flipping and fluttering in a breeze no other tree seemed to feel.

And underneath it, George: a grey wolf resting on his haunches with a wide, doggy grin on his face, tongue lolling to one side.

"George," I said sternly, "I have too far to hike today to be messing around anymore with you. Either get your butt back here and let me strap a pack to your furry hide, or leave me alone so I can get home without losing my fingers to frostbite."

I burrowed my hands deeper into my armpits, which probably would have been more effective if I'd had them under my raincoat, but that would mean opening said raincoat, which, no.

As if sensing the nearness of the end of my emotional tether, the sky very kindly hit pause on the whole snow situation.

My nose still burned with the cold.

"On second thoughts, get your furry butt over here so I can bury my face in it for a moment and warm up." My nose wrinkled. "Your fur, that is, I'm not burying my face in your butt."

George's grin didn't budge. He'd told me before that he had a hard time remembering how language worked while he was a wolf, but I squinted at him nonetheless.

"If you laugh, I'll murder you on the spot."

Happy panting.

Heaving a sigh to end all sighs, rolling my eyes hard enough that even Temporary Wolf Boy couldn't fail to read my emotions, I stomped back to the clearing where I'd left the packs.

The packs were gone.

For the splittiest of seconds, I froze again—and then because I was actually starting to freeze, I strode to the spot where the packs had lain, thin rapiers of grass still crushed and buckled in their wake, and howled, "George!!"

To his credit, he appeared almost instantly at the fringe of the clearing again, peering out between the gnarled and twisted fingers of the tea tree.

"Where," I said, "are our packs?" As if staring at him sternly with my hands on my hips would suddenly spur him to speech.

I ground my teeth.

The clouds hung above, not even a little movement in them to indicate the passing of time, no glimpse of the sunlight we'd been expecting shining through. Surely it was at least mid-morning now though, and I had, what, six hours to hike out to safety?

Fine.

Fine, I'd do it without George, without the packs—and without water I realised with a sinking stomach.

Okay.

Okay fine.

That would suck, but it was six hours, maybe seven or eight if I took it really slow to conserve energy, and sunset wasn't until... I narrowed my eyes. *I don't know, maybe five thirty, six o'clock? It was twilight when I was sitting down to dinner on Tuesday and that was...*

Sure, sunset was maybe six o'clock if I was lucky.

So I had six, maybe eight hours to walk on six, maybe seven, possibly eight hours of daylight.

Easy.

Absolutely plausible.

And it was freezing, so no doubt I'd drink less anyway. Ah ha. Ah ha-ha ha ha.

At least I'd walk faster without a pack.

www.ingramcontent.com/pod-product-compliance
Lightning Source LLC
Chambersburg PA
CBHW031257210726
48287CB00003B/1077